Published by Phoenyx Austin

Words Copyright © 2015 by Tracy Austin

Illustrations Copyright © 2015 by Tracy Austin

Website: www.DrPhoenyx.com

ISBN 978-0-9848630-4-4

Printed in the United States of America

To every beautiful brown skin girl –
May you always love your kinks and curls!

LOVE YOUR HAIR!

by PHOENYX AUSTIN, M.D.

Hey you there! Lace up your traveling shoes...

Today's a full day with lots to share!

I wrote this story for you, you, you and *you*

And why you *too* should love your hair!

So our full day first starts out with morning yoga class,

Where we enjoy a stretch and a twist...

And this I must say, is the favorite part of my day

One that surely cannot be missed!

Psst! Excuse me fellow yogi — yes you right there

Though I try so hard not to stare!

The curls, the twists, the waves, the puffs...

WOW — Love your hair!

Oh thank you so much fellow yoga buddy!

That is how I always reply...

And sometimes with compliments I do look away,

Sometimes I can be kinda shy!

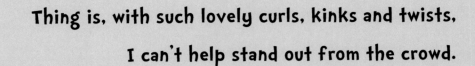

Thing is, with such lovely curls, kinks and twists,
I can't help stand out from the crowd.
Whether I choose to style my hair modestly
Or wear it big and loud!

Whether I choose to wear my hair tame or tousled
Going here or going there...
Whether it's long, short, tied, or loose
There's nothing quite like my hair!

See, my hair's got more flash than diamond earrings,

And more hipness than my ripped jeans...

More sparkle than my pink glitter lip-gloss

You ladies know what I mean!

Some say my hair's like big fluffy clouds!

And some say it's like cotton candy!

Still, however *you* choose to see it ladies,

My natural hair is *oh so dandy!*

Hey! Let's cruise this cool amusement park

Let's catch a coaster ride!

Up, down, and loop de loop...

I can't keep it all inside!

All day long I like to let my hair fly
I like to let it swoop and *sway*...
I love to let my hair be free and loose!
I love to let my hair *play!*

Now all this hair play has me quite hungry

To the kitchen, let's bake up a storm!

Pies, cakes, chocolate chip cookies!

Mmmm, so yummy and warm!

Excuse me friend — what's your hair secret?

Please tell me, I must know!

Well the *secret* is really no secret at all...

If you love it, it will grow!

See some girls prefer to wear their hair short

and some like wearing it long...

And still no matter the length *you* choose

Our hair grows healthy and strong!

So be choosey with your choice of hairstyle

And pick a hairstyle perfectly YOU.

Afro puffs, braids, locs, twists!

There's so much our hair can do!

Hey you there! Straighten your hair, child!

No hair should look like that!

Sorry ma'am, but I totally disagree—

O'nat-u-ral is where it's at!

And fact is fact, my hair doesn't and shouldn't

Always do what *others* do say

Because truth is wearing my hair o'natural

Makes for a much more interesting day!

So I dance, and I prance, and I laugh, and I love

And I keep right on rhyming...

And why you say, do I stay so upbeat?

Because my hair keeps me smiling!

Hey, I've always wanted to be a Queen Bee Beekeeper

Tend to the hive, make some money!

Look, even the worker bees love my hair

They think it's *sweeter* than honey!

Next, I think, I'll go undercover
Like a double agent or super spy...
Only problem is the bad guys always spot me,
Hmmmmm, I wonder why?!?

And after I spy, I like playing underwater adventures
I love being a majestic mermaid!

Hey look — it's my buddy Mr. Sea Turtle!

Chillin' with a glass of lemonade!

And later I'll attend a fancy fashion show
Got tons of outfits to stitch and snap...
This crazy, hectic day sure has me pooped!
I think I'll take a quick cat nap.

Oh me! Oh my! I can't believe I overslept!

If I'm late, it'll be trouble...

Ugh! Getting stuck in traffic is such a bummer

I must get there on the double!

Whew! Thank goodness I made it just on time
Strike a pose, flash a smile!
My hair is the star of this fashion show
As I strut the catwalk isle!

Yes, there is so much you can learn my friends

From embracing and loving your hair...

Like being cool, classy and confident women

These qualities can be extremely rare!

Now if you asked me to be perfectly honest

I'd be the first to admit...

I didn't always truly love my own hair,

I didn't think it was a good fit.

Big, curly, kinky, natural hair

At one point just wasn't my style.

I would've taken more "manageable" hair any day.

I wasn't a fan of hair going *WILD!*

Thankfully it didn't take me too long

To cease and stop all my doubt,

And slowly I began to see the beauty of my hair

And push all those bad thoughts out!

Also I realized something *cool* about my hair

My hair's potential is vast!

And once you see the *awesomeness* I see

You'll leave your hair worries in the past!

Because having lovely locks adorn your head

is something to be thankful for!

And once you *too* start loving your hair

Even greater things will be in store!

See every day will be full of fun adventures
With rhymes to sing along...
And with fabulous tresses along the way
The day will never go wrong!

So no matter where the day takes you ladies
Remember, your hair is your crown!
So love your hair like it deeply loves you
And your hair will never let you down!

And now we've finally reached the end of my day

And it's almost time for bed...

Got my cow jammies and pink hair bonnet on

And Sam has been walked and fed

So I hope you enjoyed my story ladies

It was such a pleasure to share!

All the things that make our hair so *COOL*

And why you *too* should *LOVE YOUR HAIR!*

THE END

Thanks so much for reading Love Your Hair! Lots of love went into every word and illustration, so if you and your little one really enjoyed my book, please take a quick second to leave an Amazon review. I'd greatly appreciate your feedback!

Also, if you'd like to inquire about ordering bulk wholesale copies of Love Your Hair, please contact customer service at shop@drphoenyx.com, and visit my FitBeauty Shop at DRPHOENYX.COM to learn about my entire line of healthy hair and body products.

Thanks again for reading and supporting Love Your Hair!

– Dr. Phoenyx

44584723R00022

Made in the USA
Middletown, DE
08 May 2019